THE AMAZING GUIDE

THE AMAZING GUIDE

A DORLING KINDERSLEY BOOK

CONTENTS

Monster Trucks! 6

Monster Jam! 8

Inside the Monster 10

Up on Top 12

Gearing Up 14

In Action 16

MEET THE MONSTERS!

Grave Digger 18

Bulldozer 20

Airborne Ranger 22

Gunslinger 24

Madusa 26

Predator 28

Prowler 30

Reptoid 32

Spider-Man 34

Wild Thang 36

Wolverine 38

Behind the Scenes 40

CRRRASH! 42

Monster Truck Roster 44

Talk the Talk:
Monster Jam Glossary 46

Index/Credits 48

MONSTER TRUCKS!

MONSTER TRUCKS look like they have pumped iron for months, strapped on tires from a cartoon, and then let a slightly insane artist paint their shells. These huge, powerful racing machines have taken America by storm! Invented by Missouri garage owner Bob Chandler in the early 1980s when he strapped big tires underneath his pickup truck and called it Bigfoot, monster trucks have grown from a backyard hobby into an international, multi-million-dollar motor sport. In this book, read about how monster trucks are built, see who drives them, and experience the thrill of the loudest race on earth.

Grrrr!

Monster trucks are painted with colorful designs, such as the wild eyes of Prowler (left), or the cemetery theme of Grave Digger.

Early races

Monster truck racing has come a long way since the first truck, Bigfoot, smashed two cars with a single blow in front of a packed house in Pontiac, Michigan. At first, trucks like Bigfoot just crushed cars at motor sports events. But soon racing became part of the fun, and trucks like Grave Digger (right) took on all opponents!

How big?

Monster trucks are about 11 feet tall and 12 feet wide and 20 feet long...as big as an elephant.

Up and over

During monster truck events, such as Monster Jam, monster trucks race each other over a short course, or they do freestyle tricks to impress judges and the fans. Weighing more than 10,000 pounds, the trucks easily crush junked cars, to the delight of thousands of screaming fans.

Monster trucks can jump more than 100 feet, or nearly the length of 14 cars side by side.

Monster truck tires are as tall as three normal tires stacked together.

Some truck!

Grave Digger is one of the most successful monster trucks. As it flies over another jump, check out the green bars. Made of tubular steel, they form the frame or "chassis" [CHASS-ee]. The body that rests atop the frame is made of fiberglass. The massive engine is mounted behind the driver, who sits behind the front wheels.

Huge tires

Standing 66 inches tall, the enormous rubber tires are what really make monster trucks stand out. Made by Goodyear and Firestone, the tires are normally used for huge fertilizer spreaders. There is enough air in one tire to blow up 10,000 balloons. Monster trucks can even float on their tires due to the buoyancy of the air.

MONSTER JAM!

QUICK! COVER YOUR EARS! Monster Jam, America's loudest, coolest, wildest motor sports event, is starting! From September through March, the best monster trucks meet at arenas and stadiums all around the United States for rip-roaring racing and high-flying, car-crushing action. More than four million people attend Monster Jam events each season to watch the trucks, meet the drivers, and even sit in the gigantic tires; millions more fans watch on TV. Across the country, more than 85 cities play host to Monster Jam events.

Enormous wheels and powerful engines help monster trucks like Spider-Man leap off ramps of dirt and fly through the air.

Wheel men

One of the coolest things about going to a Monster Jam is meeting the monster truck drivers and seeing the trucks up close. Before every event, they meet with fans, pose for pictures, and sign autographs at a "Pit Party." They also answer fans' questions about the huge machines they drive. What would you like to ask a monster truck driver?

Many thanks

Every truck has its own name, design, and personality. Most are covered with sponsors' stickers, drivers' name plates, and other decals. This truck, American Guardian, honors the men and women of the U.S. armed forces.

Dirt parade

Before every Monster Jam, all the trucks competing that night circle the arena in an ear-shattering parade (above). The yellow plastic over the front rows of seats keeps fans away from the edge for their safety.

Tons of dirt are trucked in to form the monster truck racing track. The thick white line around the edge is there to make sure safety officials know where it's safe to walk.

INSIDE THE MONSTER

You won't always find the engine of a monster truck under the hood. Monster truck engines can be in the back or front of the truck.

MONSTER TRUCKS take from three to twelve months to come to life, but when they do...cover your ears! Monster trucks are made up of a steel frame, a massive engine, a fiberglass body, and four enormous tires. The trucks actually work fine without the body, but then how would you be able to tell Predator from Prowler? It costs about $150,000 to build one of these trucks, each of which is custom made, so no two monster trucks are exactly alike.

SKELETON
A computer-designed frame of steel tubes forms the roll cage that protects the drivers.

SUPER SHOCKS
In "coil-over" shocks, a tubular coil is wound around the shock cylinder.

A great body

The overall weight of monster trucks has come down a lot since they were first built. Use of lighter, stronger metals in the frames and lighter engine parts is the main reason. A lighter truck can go faster, since the engine doesn't have as much weight to move.

Under the monster

A lot goes on underneath the frame and body of a monster truck. The two red coils shown here are rear, coil-over shocks. Between them sits the rear differential assembly, which lets the wheels turn at slightly different speeds around corners. The trucks are so high off the ground that mechanics just walk in underneath and start working.

These nitrogen-filled shocks cost about $2,000 each; each truck has four sets.

Power plant

The face of a monster truck can be fierce, fiery, or fun. But the heart of the beast is the massive engine (left). Built at a cost of more than $35,000, these eight-cylinder engines can be as large as 575 cubic inches. Compare that to a typical car engine of 280 cubic inches. The engines burn methanol, and use more than seven gallons in about two seconds to go about 250 feet.

HATS ON This large silver triangle is the injector hat, which shoots air into the engine.

FUEL UP Injector nozzles shoot fuel into the cylinders; the fuel mixes with air to cause the pistons to fire.

The heart of the wheels is the knuckle gear (inside the wheel hub) that allows the wheels to turn safely.

POWER PACK The red cylinder is the magneto, which creates electricity that helps start the engine.

PLUG IN Eight blue tubes, one for each engine cylinder, connect the spark plugs to the magneto

The last step

After a monster truck leaves the shop and is made ready for racing, one of the final steps is putting on the 66-inch tall, 43-inch wide tires. While in the shop, the trucks roll on regular tires. The red jack above is being used by the mechanic to boost the truck up enough to roll the $1,800 monster tires on.

These header tubes vent air and other gases from the engine; they look cool, too! There is one tube for each engine cylinder.

UP ON TOP

Only Grave Digger has a door on the side. On most trucks, drivers climb in from beneath the cab.

IMAGINE sitting on top of a basketball rim. That's how far above the ground Monster Jam drivers sit while driving. It's a great view from up there, with the huge crowd cheering, the dirt flying, and the truck bouncing you around like a beach ball in the surf. While it sure is fun to drive a monster truck, Monster Jam drivers also have to be highly-trained specialists with a great knowledge of their truck's driving and safety gear. Take a close-up look at the "office" of a monster truck driver.

Leadfeet only!

Like a normal car or truck, monster trucks have a gas pedal (called the "accelerator") on the right and a brake pedal on the left (below). Drivers use their feet to make the truck go and stop, but they use their eyes to watch everything going on around them, including this RPM gauge (right).

HOPE WE DON'T NEED THAT
Along with other fire safety gear, a driver has a fire extinguisher nearby just in case it is needed.

KEEP IT STRAIGHT
Made of metal and heavy-duty plastic, steering wheels are normally about 10 inches across.

NICE VIEW
Monster trucks are so big, drivers can't see what is dirctly in front of them. When driving near people, drivers rely on outside guides for safety.

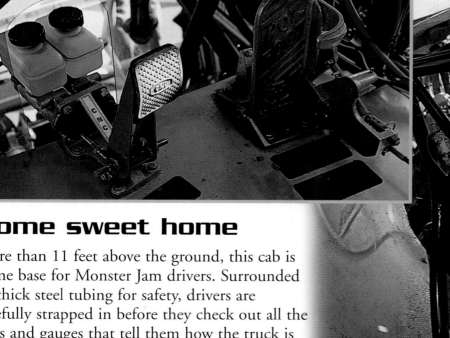

Home sweet home

More than 11 feet above the ground, this cab is home base for Monster Jam drivers. Surrounded by thick steel tubing for safety, drivers are carefully strapped in before they check out all the dials and gauges that tell them how the truck is running. Oh, yes, one more thing: Did we mention that you can see through the floor?!

In control

Each truck has switches, dials, gauges, and levers that help the driver control the truck and make sure the engine is running safely and well. The white switches operate the ignition, fan, fuel pump, water pump, and lights. The silver handle with the white ball on top is the locking shift lever. While steering with one hand, drivers use their right hand to shift through three gears.

CLICK, CLICK Drivers don't usually use these switches during a race. They're too busy just steering!

Super safe

Sometimes a driver has to shut off his truck's engine very quickly, such as during a rollover or a crash. There are three ways to shut off the truck: a pull-ring on the back; a button located within reach of the driver; and a radio switch (called the RII) operated by a track official. Before every race, drivers test all these devices.

DRIVERS' EYE VIEW

At the 2001 Monster Finals in Las Vegas, some monster truck drivers spoke about life behind the wheel.

Q. What's your favorite thing about driving monster trucks?

JILL CANUSO, WRENCHEAD.COM:

The most fun thing is the flying part. I love that the best. It feels like you're taking off in an airplane. When the wheels leave the ground you have a floating feeling. Of course, then you have to land! That's not always the fun part.

TONY FARRELL, WILD THANG:

I like the driving, but I love the Pit Parties where you meet the fans face to face. They're the ones that this is all about. Without them, none of us would be here.

CHARLIE PAUKEN, GRAVE DIGGER 7:

It's a blast, a great adrenalin rush. It's like riding a roller coaster, except I'm driving the roller coaster!

Q. How did you get started driving monster trucks?

MADUSA:

I raced dirt bikes and ATVs, I'm always been sort of a tomboy. And my 78-year-old grandmother rides a Harley [motorcycle]. I've always loved driving and racing.

Q. What happens before a race?

JILL CANUSO:

First, you check your emergency radio shut-off. Then the starter lines you up on the starting line. You give him the thumbs up and wait for the green light. At the green, you give it throttle and go!

GEARING UP

WHEN DRIVERS first climbed into monster trucks, they wore T-shirts, baseball caps, and sneakers. But just as the trucks have gotten bigger and faster and use more technology, drivers' gear has improved dramatically, too. The main purpose of everything the drivers wear is safety. In case of an accident or a fire, the drivers' clothes may be what saves them from injury. Of course, the logo-covered racing suits still look pretty cool, too!

Basic gear

Monster Jam drivers have many pieces of safety equipment available to them. All drivers must wear a helmet and gloves and special safety shoes, as well as a thick foam neck collar below their helmet to keep their head from bobbing around too much. Some drivers also wear thick canvas and elastic "kidney belts" under their racing suits to help them absorb impact.

HANDS DOWN Some drivers' gloves are leather on the outside and Nomex (flameproof fabric) on the inside for fire safety.

Tools of the trade

Drivers and team members need special equipment before a race, such as the wrench used by Gunslinger driver Scott Hartsock (below). That's why team trailers are actually complete rolling garages (above).

TIGHTEN UP Belts like these help drivers deal with the pounding they go through in a race.

Lookin' good

While the drivers suit up in fancy colored outfits that fans love, even the trucks themselves get snazzed up for the show. Truck paint is spruced up, and special tire foam is sprayed on the wheels so that the rubber will shine under the lights.

Working clothes

Gunslinger driver Scott Hartsock models the racing suit that was specially designed for Monster Jam drivers by Deist Safety Co. The lightweight suits are made from three layers of high-tech fire-resistant fabric: Nomex, Kevlar, and Carbonex. These types of fabric give a driver time to escape a fire safely by keeping the heat from reaching his or her skin. The suits are strapped tight around the neck with velcro. Drivers also wear helmets and gloves.

Heads up

The helmet is the drivers' most important piece of safety equipment. Under a fiberglass shell pained with team logos, the helmet is made of Kevlar, the same materials used in bulletproof vests. Some Monster Jam drivers use a full face guard that protects their jaw, too. Under the helmets, drivers wear a headsock made of fire-resistant Nomex. Tiny headphones in each ear help them communicate with pit crews.

PATCHES Drivers' suits are decorated with the team logo and the logos of sponsors.

TEAM COLORS Like the uniform of a sports team, a driver and his crew all wear the same color and design.

TIGHT HANDS So that no air or fire can slip in, wrist cuffs are made to fit very snugly.

NO JEANS All driver suits include full-length pants that cover the top of the driving boots.

BOOTS Drivers wear specially made driving boots that are leather outside with a Kevlar layer inside.

Fans dress up, too

Trucks and drivers aren't the only ones who dress up for Monster Jam events. Fans wear T-shirts, hats, bandannas, and more to show support for their favorites. Kids like to get their hair and faces painted, too!

15

MONSTER ACTION!

READY, SET, GO! And the monster trucks are off on another dirt-churnin', ear-rattlin', pulse-poundin' ride down the track and over the crushed cars. That's how monster trucks race, and the pictures on these pages show some of those races. At a Monster Jam show, you might see trucks doing all these things...plus a whole lot more. The massive, fuel-eating engines of these trucks have got to let off a little steam!

Inside the monsters

While the powerful engines and enormous tires of monster trucks do the dirty work, Monster Jam drivers are the brains behind all the noise. Predator driver Allen Pezo waves to the crowd after finishing up one of his runs. Notice the thick collar he wears to protect his neck from the car-smashing shocks.

Viva El Toro Loco! The name of this cousin of Bulldozer means "The Crazy Bull" in Spanish.

Grippers

Monster truck tires have a much wider and deeper "tread" than regular tires. The tread is the pattern of raised ridges that help the tires grab the dirt. Some drivers shave off hundreds of pounds of rubber to make the tires lighter.

A dusty flight

Monster Jam arenas use moist soil that is good for the big tires to get a grip on. But drivers sometimes like to take their trucks out into empty fields (or even their backyards!) and kick up a little dust, like El Toro Loco does here.

Gettin' big air!

Another great event at Monster Jam is freestyle. Individual trucks get free rein on the course to speed, jump, pound, crash, spin, and just generally go nuts, thrilling their screaming fans. The trucks can really get up there; in this shot, the front of the truck is more than 25 feet above the arena floor.

Head to head

One type of racing at Monster Jam events is head-to-head racing around a "J-turn" course. The trucks take off from a standing start and race each other down a straightaway, then make a J-turn toward a line of cars waiting to be crushed. The races demand skill and timing from the driver and power from the truck. The winner is the first truck to cross the finish line.

Look out below!

Wouldn't you like to be able to do this the next time you got stuck in traffic with your mom or dad? Good thing there is no one inside those crushed cars below Gunslinger, or they'd be flatter than pancakes. Each Monster Jam show smashes into smithereens anywhere from 18 to 25 cars and other vehicles.

Go for distance

During a race, monster trucks go faster through the air than they do rolling over cars. So drivers try to make their jumps as long as possible. In this sequence, Eradicator clears six cars before it lands, a jump of more than 40 feet! Drivers can't steer once they're airborne...they just have to gun it and hope!

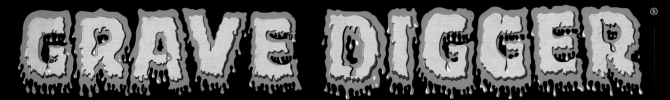

GRAVE DIGGER ®

IF MONSTER JAM has a Number One Star, then most fans would agree that star is Grave Digger. Since the early 1980s, Grave Digger has been crushing cars, steamrolling past racing opponents, and thrilling audiences with show after show of daredevil action. Driver Dennis Anderson has created a legend and won a legion of fans with his take-no-prisoners style.

Look out!

Anderson often takes Grave Digger over jumps at top speed, meaning that when he lands...he sometimes just can't stop! It's a good thing that there have been more than a dozen Grave Digger trucks over the years. Much of the Grave Digger truck evolution has been in the hands of Dennis Anderson, together with Paul "Pablo" Huffaker. Anderson built the original truck, but Pablo takes credit for building Diggers #4, #10, #11, #12—and another one is on the drawing board.

TOMBSTONES Painted on Grave Digger's side are grave markers with the names of trucks it has defeated.

STARING EYES
Among Digger's trademarks are the evil-looking red headlights that signal its arrival.

Digger power!

Grave Digger's driver Dennis Anderson loves to "get air." He spends so much time sending his 10,000-pound truck flying over obstacles and jumps that he should have a pilots' license!

Here's Gary Porter, another one of Grave Digger's drivers, holding a Grave Digger toy. All the "Digger Drivers" drive in the style of Dennis Anderson.

Dirt on Digger

➤ Grave Digger's body is modeled after a 1950 Chevy panel truck.

➤ Dennis Anderson started out in mud-bogging; he was called Grave Digger long before he built his first monster truck.

➤ Grave Digger #12 is two feet longer and five inches wider than previous Grave Diggers.

➤ Grave Digger's crashes mean thousands of dollars in repairs. Each Grave Digger body is a one-of-a-kind masterpiece!

Air-brush artist Jim McShea custom paints each Grave Digger, including repainting them after every crash!

BULLDOZER®

'Dozer Details

➤ *Driver Guy Wood is an expert carpenter; he built his kids a three-story treehouse!*

➤ *Bulldozer's smoking nostrils are really blowing harmless carbon dioxide (CO_2) gas.*

➤ *Its body is based on a Chevy.*

➤ *Bulldozer's "cousin" is El Toro Loco, which means "The Crazy Bull" in Spanish.*

USUALLY, WHEN A BULL sees red, it charges! But Bulldozer makes its ear-rattling, ground-pounding, dirt-churning charge when it sees *green*...a green light at the start of a Monster Jam race, that is. Driven by veteran wheelman Guy Wood, Bulldozer is one of the most unique-looking and powerful monster trucks going. Beneath Bulldozer's 1,500 horsepower, 572 cubic-inch aluminum Rodeck engine and its nasty-looking horns, this monster truck packs more punch than a truckload of real bulls.

DECALS Trucks wear stickers. These ones are for the U.S. Hot Rod Association and event promoter SFX.

Attention to detail

Bulldozer's unique paint job is so detailed, if you get up close it even looks like as if he is covered with fine brown hair. The truck comes complete with a silver ring through the bull's nostrils (that's where the snorting smoke comes from) and enormous horns set atop the cab.

ONE DOWN, THREE TO GO Monster trucks are so well balanced, they can run on three wheels.

Climb the ladder

When lining up to crush cars in the freestyle events, monster trucks don't always go fast and jump. Sometimes, they roll up slowly and then just drive up and over. It takes practice to learn just when to gun the motor to go over.

Bulldozer's not smiling...that's a look of grim determination to win!

SHOCKING
Bulldozer uses nitrogen shocks to support the force of 10,000 pounds of "bull."

Teeth-rattlin'

Above each of Bulldozer's 66-inch-tall front wheels, you can see a row of teeth...just like an scowling bull. Guy Wood and his team say that the truck and its teeth take such a pounding from jumps like this one that they sometimes feel more like dentists that monster truck mechanics!

AIRBORNE RANGER ™

IT'S HARD ENOUGH to control a 10,000-pound monster truck with both arms and both legs. Joe Cypher does it with just his hands! Joe lost the use of his legs after a car accident twelve years ago. Away from his truck, he uses a wheelchair to get around. But he loved racing, so he created the first monster truck controlled by hand. "Ranger Joe," as he is known, uses special hand levers to work the brakes, throttle, and safety gear of Airborne Ranger.

Unstoppable

Joe Cypher's determination has been an inspiration to many fans. He hasn't let his disability stop him from achieving his dreams. When fans at Monster Jam events see that red, white, and blue U.S. flag waving from the back end of a high-flying Airborne Ranger, they realize that they're watching a real American hero.

MAKE ROOM
Airborne Ranger's body is cut high above the tires to allow for its huge wheel travel.

SALUTE!
Airborne Ranger is decorated on both sides with a battle-scarred American flag.

Power plant

Take a good look at Airborne Ranger's massive engine as Joe Cypher pops a huge wheelie. Ranger boasts a 510 cubic-inch Chevy Bow Tie 8/71 Motor and a modified "Art Carr" Turbo 400 transmission. The truck's body is a 2000 Chevy Super Truck model, made of fiberglass. Joe also uses the standard 66-inch-tall, 45-inch-wide monster truck tires.

With a press of the gas, Airborne Ranger's nose flips up to pull a spectacular wheelie!

Though he does not have the use of his legs, "Ranger Joe" Cypher has not let that stop him from becoming all that he can be.

Ranger Report

➤ Driver Joe Cypher has also been a champion wheelchair basketball player and wheelchair arm wrestler.

➤ Joe dedicated his truck to the U.S. Army Airborne Rangers, a unit that is always among the first to defend the nation.

➤ The next monster truck that Joe builds will come complete with a wheelchair lift to give kids with disabilities the chance to sit in the driver's seat.

GUN SLINGER™

LIKE A GUNFIGHTER in the Old West, Gunslinger is ready to take on all challengers. Also like those old-time warriors, driver Scott Hartsock started out as a lone gun; he and his wife developed Gunslinger themselves and sold the first sponsorships that put them on the road to Monster Jam. Today, Gunslinger is one of the circuit's most feared trucks.

Turn, turn, turn

Like all monster trucks, Gunslinger's main steering is through the front wheels. But drivers can also make the back wheels turn by throwing a switch in the cab. This allows the trucks to make it around very tight turns in a race or even to spin dirt-churnin' donuts.

Let me hear you!

Driver Scott Hartsock says his favorite thing about monster truck racing is hearing the cheers of his fans. He also says that the most important thing a driver needs is dedication—"Without that, you won't last very long in this game."

HEADS UP Monster truck drivers are so strapped-in that they often can't see what they're landing on.

On the road

Gunslinger's making a 100-foot trip over a row of cars in this photo, but in the course of a Monster Jam season, the truck will travel much farther than that. Driver Scott Hartsock and his team will travel more than 60,000 miles between races and their home base in Florida.

WHY BLUE? The cars that monster trucks crush are painted bright colors so that they look cool for fans.

STOCK TRUCK Gunslinger's fiberglass body is molded after an actual Ford F150 pickup truck.

Below, Gunslinger launches itself over five—count 'em!—yellow junkers. The flying looks like fun, but drivers will tell you the landing's are no picnic. Even though they are protected by safety gear, drivers still get rattled around when they hit the ground.

Gunslinger Guide

➤ Driver Scott Hartsock chose the name Gunslinger for his truck because he's a gunsmith by profession.

➤ Scott and his crew travel from race to race in a custom-built trailer with room for the truck and for sleeping.

➤ Scott has some advice for anyone who wants to become a monster truck driver: 1. Build a truck (make sure to follow the rules); 2. Get a sponsor; 3. Drive!; 4. Dedicate yourself to it!

MADUSA™

AMERICAN GIRLS have a new role model—and she drives around on top of 10,000 pounds of dirt-churnin' metal! Madusa roared onto the Monster Jam scene a few years ago and quickly proved that she belonged. As one of the only female drivers on the scene, she had a tough road. But she impressed everyone with her hard work and her thrill-seeking freestyle performances. "I love seeing all the little girls at the shows!" beams Madusa.

Mad About Madusa
➤ Not only is Madusa a famous Monster Jam driver, but she's a longtime professional wrestler. She also competed in kickboxing in Japan and Thailand.

➤ Before she started driving monster trucks, Madusa built and raced motorcycles. She even goes riding with her 78-year-old grandmother!

➤ Madusa has appeared in movies and her own workout video.

LOOK FAMILIAR? Madusa the truck is modeled after the popular Ford F-150 pickup style.

Face front

Because Madusa the driver is better known than Madusa the truck, it only makes sense that she gets to have her picture on the hood of the truck. Want to know how the star-spangled wrestler-turned-driver got her name? She shortened the slogan "Made in the USA."

Learn from the best

Madusa went to North Carolina to train for her first monster truck race at the home of Dennis Anderson, driver of the world-famous Grave Digger.

GOOD GRIP Many drivers shave their tire treads into sharp edges; they call them "meat hooks."

Patriotic paint

Madusa has always used red, white, and blue in her wrestling uniforms. So when it came time to design the look of her monster truck, those American colors were an obvious choice. Her fans streak their hair with the familiar colors, too.

Style points

Madusa's best event is the freestyle. At the first Monster Jam World Finals in Las Vegas, she did an "endo" over an ice-cream truck and flipped the truck completely over! But she got out to the roar of the crowd. "You should have heard those fans when I got out; it was awesome!" That's what she loves best, entertaining people.

PREDATOR

IN THE ANIMAL kingdom, a predator is feared by all the other animals. In Monster Jam, Predator is one of the most feared opponents. Fans know when they see Predator's glaring yellow eyes and gleaming white fangs that they are in for a roaring good time.

BIG DROP
"Wheel drop" measures how far the suspension drops during a jump.

GRRRR!
Why Predator? "Because I want my truck to prey on cars!" says driver Allen Pezo.

Head to head

Here's Predator going nose to nose with a competitor in a race. Both trucks are flying through the air. Looks like Predator might win this battle by a fang!

Predator looks as mean as its engine sounds!

PREDATOR PAWS
Predator's tires stand more than five feet tall!

Predator skeleton

This tightly-welded, all-steel undercarriage supports Predator's massive engine. The scientifically designed chassis [CHASS-ee] is like a real predator's skeleton, providing the truck the support it needs to handle the pressure created when Predator lands "feet" first onto a row of cars.

PROWLER™

LOOK FAMILIAR? It should. The growling Prowler is a cousin to Predator. Prowler is modeled after the big cats that "prowl" the jungle, looking for their next meal. Prowler the truck makes meals out of other monster trucks, revving a massive engine to create a different kind of roar. Can you imagine what a tiger the size of an elephant might sound like? Now you don't have to imagine—you can just listen to Prowler's growler!

EARS TO YOU
Prowler's "ears" could double as rear-view mirrors... if these trucks had mirrors!

CUSTOM MADE
Prowler's fiberglass body is custom made from a special mold.

Ready to rock

Before Monster Jam shows, monster trucks and their drivers wait in "pit" areas before they enter the racing arena. In the pits, they tune their engines and make sure their fire suits are fitted securely and their safety belts are strapped on tightly. They also make sure the truck itself is clean and shiny. The arena or stadium lights should gleam off the highlights of the truck, like Prowler's bright yellow eyes. The impact-resistant windshield (made of Lexan) is carefully cleaned. Not only does this look good, but it ensures the driver can see where he's going!

HOW HIGH? When doing wheelies and jumps, monster trucks can fly as high as 30 feet.

The en-"tire" story

Monster Jam drivers say that the one thing fans want to know about more than anything else is how much the tires cost. Well, it's a good thing that mom and dad don't have to get four of these 66-inchers for the family van (though that would be cool, wouldn't it?). Each of the tires can cost nearly $2,000 brand-new. That's $8,000 per truck. Plus, monster trucks keep lots of spare tires on hand.

A toothy smile!

Prowler may look a little like a cartoon tiger, but he's anything but funny! Prowler's unique custom-made body sports two-foot-long teeth at the front, along with carefully-painted "tiger" facial features, making a ride in this truck a real "jungle cruise." The tiger stripes go all around the back of the truck. About the only thing that's missing from this 1,600 horsepower big cat is a tail. But when it's runnin' good, that's about all opposing drivers see of Prowler—the back end!

Prowler's Growls

➤ Underneath the gleaming eyes on Prowler's hood is a massive 557 cubic-inch, eight-cylinder engine that makes for one enormous roar!

➤ Many monster truck drivers come to Monster Jam from other motor sports, such as drag racing or mud-bogging.

➤ The new man behind Prowler's wheel is driver Larry Jarzel.

REPTOID™

KIDS LOVE DINOSAURS. Everyone knows that. Kids also love monster trucks. So when driver/owner Jim Jack was looking for a unique design for his new monster truck, he and designer Steve Hills took the best of both worlds and created a living, breathing dinosaur-lizard-truck that has become one of the fans' favorites. Reptoid's intricate paint job, including red, green, and magenta scales, mimics the skin patterns of some lizards. But where they got those nasty-looking teeth from is anybody's guess!

I SEE YOU Monster trucks don't have side windows, both for safety and to let drivers wave to the fans.

Flying lizard

Very few reptiles can fly, of course. Most of them stick close to the ground and the water. Jim Jack remembers one race when his truck's ability in the wet stuff proved to be a winner. "It rained before and during a show at the Los Angeles Coliseun," Jack says. "The track was soaking wet and turned into a big mud bog. But I guess being a 'reptile' helped, because I beat all the other trucks in that swamp!"

WHITE OUT Monster Jam drivers like to smash big cars like Cadillacs. Big cars...big noise!

PSSSS! Reptoid shoots out a blast of CO2 gas, making the truck look like a smokin' dragon.

DON'T SCRATCH THE PAINT It can cost more than $3,000 to repaint Reptoid.

Up and over

During the head-to-head racing portion of every Monster Jam show, drivers try to spend as much time in the air as they can. Their trucks move faster during jumps than they do driving on straightaways. That's why you see many monster trucks "fly" over the white-chalk finish line rather than drive over it.

Gas up

Reptoid uses nitrogen gas shock absorbers (vertical silver rods, above). The compression of the gas within the cylinders makes for better control and stability while the truck is bouncing up and down like an out-of-control beach ball! Most monster trucks now use these high-tech devices.

Reptoid Report

➤ Reptoid went through 26 transmissions before the team settled on the Lenco 3-speed.

➤ One of Reptoid's most important crew members is Jim Jack's wife, Linda.

➤ "The best part of racing is winning," says Jack. "There's nothing like the feeling you get when you run as hard as you can and then you win!"

SPIDER-MAN®

AFTER THEY GET a look at Spider-Man's outrageous design and listen to the powerful engine, other monster truck drivers probably wish that he'd go back to comic books! One of Monster Jam's newest entries is this cool truck modeled after the famous Marvel Comics Super Hero, your "friendly neighborhood Spider-Man." But on the track, he's anything but friendly, going all out to defeat his rivals—except the truck does it with horse power, not spider-power!

Overhead

In the comic book, Spider-Man can't fly; he uses web strands to swing from place to place. But in Monster Jam, Spider-Man *can* fly! He just gets that massive engine roaring at high revs and takes off, with all four wheels off the ground. Look out below!

STRENGTH! Spider-Man with two legs can lift school buses. Spider-Man with wheels crushes them!

Body news

Spider-Man's sleek fiberglass body is made from a custom mold and painted with the same colors as the comic-book character's costume. On the back of the truck is a huge web design... just perfect for snaring unsuspecting fellow monster truck drivers!

POWERHOUSE
"Spidey's" engine is a 1,500 horsepower, 540 cubic-inch Richard Midgette motor.

TRANNY
Spider-Man uses a Dedenbear 2-speed transmission by Coan.

Spider-Man can't shoot web out of this truck, but he can use his great acceleration to "shoot" from the starting gate!

MARVEL

WILD THANG ™

ALL THE MONSTER JAM trucks sport cool designs, wild body types, and one-of-a-kind paint jobs. But Wild Thang just might be the most unique of all. Created by the weird minds of Brian Ashley and driver Tony Farrell, the best way to describe this custom-made monster is to call it an orange skull with sunglasses and a spider crawling out of the back. You won't see anything like this driving into the local mall! Wild Thang's original mold cost $20,000 to make; new bodies can be molded for another $5,000 each.

Thang Things

➤ Wild Thang creator and driver Tony Farrell drives a school bus in his spare time. He's the only Monster Jam driver who drives one bus and crushes others! How'd you like to see him driving your school bus?

➤ The kids on Tony's school bus helped choose the design for Wild Thang.

➤ Tony was a champion mud racer for 10 years before turning to monster trucks.

YUCK! The red bits are the nasty-looking gums of Wild Thang's "mouth." Time to visit the dentist!

LOOKIN' COOL Yep, those are sunglasses Wild Thang is wearing. Just perfect for those bright arena lights!

Not just a pretty face

Underneath its pretty smile, Wild Thang has a powerhouse engine! On top of the 66-inch tall, 43-inch wide tires, the truck boasts a 557 cubic-inch, 1,400-horsepower Chevy engine. Its Turbo 400 transmission really helps it get up and go. Farrell constructed the custom chassis in his home garage in Indiana.

Say cheese!

Wild Thang boasts a set of choppers that would make any dentist proud. Bright and white (though some are stained with blood), they tell the competition that the weirdest-looking truck in Monster Jam events is ready for action!

Wild Thang has a giant spider crawling out of a "hole" in its skull. It also has a bright purple suspension system.

Keep it fair

Like all Monster Jam trucks, Wild Thang might look, well, wild, but it's built carefully to comply with the rules that keep the races fair. The U.S. Hot Rod Association checks each truck to make sure that the engines, transmissions, and other mechanical parts meet the competition specs. USHRA officials also help ensure driver safety.

WOLVERINE®

IT'S HARD TO SAY who is more powerful: the mutant Super Hero named Wolverine or the 1,500-horsepower monster truck named Wolverine. The truck outweighs the comic-book star by 10,000 pounds, but it doesn't have claws made of unbreakable admantium. Of course, the mutant Wolverine can't go from 0 to 50 in less than three seconds, he can't squash a bus like a bug, and he doesn't make 30,000 people scream with joy as he finishes off another winning race. So, you make the call!

Fixer uppers

One of Marvel Comics' most popular stars, Wolverine has the mutant ability to heal himself rapidly. However, Wolverine the truck depends, like other Monster Jam trucks, on a highly-trained crew of mechanics and engineers to keep it running.

HEAVY DUTY
It would take about six of you to equal the weight of one 600-pound tire.

Wonderin' about Wolverine

➤ If it has wheels, Wolverine driver Brian Barthel has probably raced it. Along with formerly driving Monster Jam's Little Tiger, Brian has raced motorcycles, three-wheelers, and dragsters. He's even raced boats!

➤ In the Marvel comic books, Wolverine is a member of the incredible X-Men, a team of mutants who battle the forces of evil.

SHARP! These molded silver "claws" look like the real claws that spring from Wolverine's hands.

Danger sign

See the red light near the top of the windshield? That means that Wolverine's RII safety gear is operational. Track officials can see that light from their safety station so they can turn off the engine in case of a crash or other trouble. The red light also means Wolverine is in the right-hand lane for this race.

VRROOOM! The 540 cubic-inch engine was created by Richard Midgette with a Merlin block.

Look sharp!

Wolverine is a customized 2001 Chevy truck. Side flaps on the cab imitate the headgear sported by Wolverine himself and the colors match the original Wolverine costume. Of course, the comic Wolverine doesn't come with 66-inch tires!

BEHIND THE SCENES

MONSTER JAM EVENTS are held in front of thousands of people at stadiums and arenas. But there is much more to the event going on behind the scenes. While you're in the parking lot or at the Pit Party checking out the trucks up close, dozens of people are working long, hard hours to make the thrilling, high-jumping, non-stop action happen. Mechanics prepare the trucks; drivers train and perfect their skills; stadium workers get the place ready for fans; track workers set up the jumps, ramps, and obstacles; and fans line up, anxiously awaiting their chance to feel the roar!

Take five: Gunslinger driver Scott Hartsock grabs a little shut-eye in his trailer before climbing into the cab for his race.

Pit Party!

Before most Monster Jam shows, fans can take part in the Pit Party held outside the arena. The monster trucks at the show line up and fans can check them out up close. Drivers are available for autographs and to pose for pictures.

Final check

Predator driver Allen Pezo carefully checks out his truck before he gets ready to race. All the Monster Jam drivers are also truck and engine experts. They know their machines inside and out. The more the driver can contribute to working on the truck, the more success the team will have on the track.

Tunnel time

Most stadiums and arenas have huge entry tunnels like this one at Tampa's Raymond James Stadium. The trucks wait in high-ceilinged spaces beneath the seats for their turn to race. Track officials signal each driver when it's his turn to guide the truck out onto the track. For drivers, waiting in this tunnel is like a football player waiting to charge out onto the field. They are nervous...but very excited about getting the chance to stomp on it!

Two trucks in one

Monster trucks can't drive themselves from event to event. For one thing, they are too big to legally hit the streets. For another, they get terrible gas mileage! Teams transport their monster trucks inside huge 18-wheel trailers that also house complete mechanics' workshops.

Soon to be smashed

At each track, stadium workers prepare the course that the monster trucks will race over. Monster trucks can crush cars, buses, vans, trailers, and even motor homes during their freestyle performances. The junkers' batteries and glass are removed for safety before crushing begins.

Don't forget the wheels!

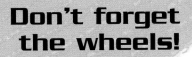

In the hours before race time, while fans are meeting drivers and workers are preparing the track, drivers and mechanics work hard on their trucks. They make sure that when the green light goes on, the trucks are in tip-top condition.

CRRRASH!

THE OBJECT OF monster truck races is to finish first; the goal in freestyle is to score the most points. But along the way, well, things happen. Sometimes drivers lose control of their massive, high-speed, high-flying machines and the result can be a spectacular rollover. But while the trucks generally don't look too good after a crash, safety gear and clothing make sure that drivers get to walk away, shaken up but not hurt.

One on one

At the Monster Jam World Finals in March, 2001, two Monster Jam trucks ended up out of action—and the crowd loved it! Dennis Anderson brought out three Grave Diggers and turned 'em all upside down. Tom Meents smashed up a pair of his trucks, including one that flipped over (bottom).

DON'T PARK THERE
Believe it or not, that pile of debris used to be a fully-stocked motor home.

STEEL CAGE
Drivers are surrounded top and bottom by thick steel cages for complete protection.

Headin' down

The wheels are designed to take a pounding, but sometimes things go a little too far and a wheel snaps off the axles—as Avenger shows. Did you know the trucks can still move on three wheels?

Time to cheer!

As safety crews rush to make sure the driver is okay, he often beats them to the punch by leaping out of the cab and raising his arms. Once the crowd knows the driver is okay, he gets a huge round of applause. Drivers would rather get those cheers for winning, but they'll take 'em for surviving.

QUICK HELP
Dodging flying tires and debris, track officials quickly move to the truck to aid the driver.

Tom Wood Ford
96th & Keystone
846-4241

M.J. ROSTER

FROM **AIRBORNE RANGER** to Wolverine, here are the Monster Jam trucks. New trucks are added regularly, so make sure to visit the Monster Jam website at www.ushra.com.

AIRBORNE RANGER™

BUSTIN' LOOSE™

DESTROYER™

EL TORO LOCO™

KING KRUNCH™

MADUSA™

MOUNTAINEER™

PROWLER™

REPTOID™

SUDDEN IMPACT™

SURVIVOR™

THRASHER™

WILD THANG™

AMERICAN GUARDIAN™

AVENGER™

BULLDOZER®

ERADICATOR™

GRAVE DIGGER®

GUNSLINGER™

PREDATOR®

SPIDER-MAN®

WOLVERINE®

MONSTER JAM®

United States
HOT ROD
Association®

TALK THE TALK

"Man, did you see that truck do a donut and then a wheelie before it got air! I was afraid he was gonna lose fire or have to pull the pin!"

Did you understand that? If you did, then consider yourself a serious Monster Jam gearhead. If you didn't, then read on to learn all the cool, insider's language that real Monster Jam fans, drivers, and mechanics use everyday.

Bite

Drivers want their trucks to bite, or grip the track well. "Good hookin' clay helps the huge tires get good bite."

Cubes

Short for "cubic inches," which is how engine size is measured. A cubic inch is a square that is one inch tall, one inch wide, and one inch deep. Monster trucks can be as big as 575 "cubes."

Wheelie

Cut Tires

Each driver has his own favorite way of preparing his tires for each track. Using large, sharp tire cutting tools, they shave off hundreds of pounds of rubber to create just the right tread. They might even do it between races. Shaving off just some of the rubber creates sharp, triangular treads called MEAT HOOKS that really grip the dirt. Drivers who want to do some fancy spinning or sliding shave off nearly the entire tread, creating ONION SKINS.

Donut

When a truck spins in a circle over and over on the arena or stadium floor. The circles in the dirt look like donuts.

Cut Tires with Meat Hooks

Endo

A crash when the truck rolls end over end, as opposed to rolling on its side.

E.T.

No, not the guy from the movie. In Monster Jam events, this stands for "elapsed time," or the time a Monster Jam truck takes to finish a course on the track.

Eyeball

To inspect or check out a track before a race, or to stare down the trucks of opposing drivers.

4-link

Short name for the "four-link suspension system" that monster trucks use. Specially designed for these massive machines, 4-link helps absorb the pounding and carry the weight during races and freestyle.

Full lugs

When they leave the treads pretty much as they are, the tires are called this. (See "cut tires.")

Get Air

When a truck leaves the ground completely. "Did you see Bulldozer get air off that last jump?"

Gettin' Air

Good hookin' clay

Dirt on a track that makes it easy for Monster Jam tires to dig in and give drivers good traction for a race.

Grab a footfull

To really stomp on the accelerator, usually at the start of a race, to get a sudden, intense burst of acceleration. "When that green light goes on, I'm going to grab a footfull."

Hook Up

To dig tires into the dirt or mud and take off very quickly from the starting line. "I've got to really hook up if I'm going to beat Grave Digger."

Hot shoe

A nickname for any top driver. "Boy, Dennis Anderson's having a great day today at the Monster Jam. He's a real hot shoe!"

Lose fire

When the engine runs too hot and stalls, shutting off by itself, without help (or choice!) from the driver.

Planetary

Shorthand name for the all-important planetary gear. One of these is inside each monster truck wheel; the gearing allows for power from the axle to be transferred safely to the wheel itself.

Pole

The number one qualifying position for the start of a Monster Jam race.

Power Out

This term is used when a monster trucks rides on two wheels, or even one wheel, for a few seconds, before the driver uses acceleration and some fancy steering to keep his truck upright.

Pull the pin

Safety is very important in Monster Jam events. When a truck rolls over, a track official can pull a red ring out of a device on the back of the truck, automatically shutting off the engine.

Red light

At the start of a race, monster truck drivers must wait for a green light before they can "grab a footfull." If they jam on the accelerator during the red light (before the green light goes on), they will be disqualified, which means their time won't count in the results.

Revs

Short for "revolutions per minute" (RPM). The higher the RPM, the faster an engine "turns over" and the faster the truck can go (up to the limits of the rules, of course). Monster Jam trucks can go above 8,000 RPM.

RII

Pronounced "arr-eye-eye," this is the initials for the remote ignition interrupter, a radio-controlled safety device that shuts off the engine in a crash. Track officials carry the radio and send a signal to the truck in case of a rollover or smash-up.

Roundy-round

A particular kind of monster truck racing course that has two turns, making it roughly circular in shape.

Staging

Staging

Track officials carefully line up each monster truck on the starting line. This is called "staging the trucks."

Wheel travel

The distance the wheels can move up and down the length of the shocks. Cars have six or eight inches; monster trucks up to 30 inches!

INDEX

American Guardian 9
Anderson, Dennis 18-19, 27, 43, 47
Ashley, Brian 36
Attendance, Monster Jam events 8
Avenger 43

Barthel, Brian 38
Bigfoot 6
Bulldozer 20-21, 46

Cab, parts of 12-13
Canuso, Jill 13
Chandler, Bob 6

El Toro Loco 16
Engines, parts of 10-11
Eradicator 17

Farrell, Tony 13, 36-37
Freestyle competition 17, 27

Grave Digger 7, 12-13, 18-19, 27, 42, 47
Gunslinger 14, 17, 24-25

Hartsock, Scott 14-15, 24-25, 42
Helmets 15
Huffaker, Paul "Pablo" 18

Jack, Jim 32-33

Los Angeles Coliseum 32

Madusa 13, 26-27
McShea, Jim 19

Monster Jam World Finals 2001 19, 27

O'Donnell, Lee 34

Pauken, Charlie 13
Pezo, Allen 16, 28, 42
Pit Party 8, 42
Predator 6, 10, 16, 28-29
Prowler 10, 30-31

Racing suits 15
Raymond James Stadium 41
Reptoid 32-33
RII switch 13, 39, 47

Safety gear 14-15, 42
Safety officials 9, 43
Shocks 10, 21, 33
Size, monster trucks 6
Spider-Man 8, 34-35

Tires
    cleaning 14
    shaving down 16, 22, 27
    size of 7, 29, 36, 38
    treads 16

USHRA 34, 41

Wild Thang 36-37
Wolverine 38-39
Wood, Guy 20-21
Wrenchead.com 13

X-Men 38

ACKNOWLEDGEMENTS

The publishers and the Shoreline Publishing Group would like to thank the many people without whose help this book would not have been possible...or as good.

LCI's Liza Abrams, Wally Cabrera, and Evelyn Caceres were invaluable in providing background information on the trucks, as well as helping design the roster of trucks on pages 44-45.

From SFX and Monster Jam itself, thanks to Denise Haller, an enthusiastic and extremely helpful supporter of the project from the beginning.

Thanks also to Mike Wales, who was so generous with his time and expertise at the Monster Jam World Finals, along with the many drivers, engineers, and crew members we interviewed for this book. Thanks to Tina Huffaker for her help with photographs.

Special thanks to Pete Samek and Andy Christie of Slim Films in New York for their rockin' photo-illustration masterpieces on the cover and on pages 16-38. Also thanks to photographer Al Messerschmidt for his behind-the-scenes work.

LONDON, NEW YORK, SYDNEY, DELHI, PARIS, MUNICH and JOHANNESBURG

Produced by
Shoreline Publishing Group
Editorial Director and
"Monster Jam" Writer
James Buckley, Jr.
Art Director Thomas J. Carling, Carling Design Inc.
Photo-illustrations Slim Films

For Dorling Kindersley
Design Concept Lisa Lanzarini
Art Director Cathy Tincknell
Publishing Manager Cynthia O'Neill
Senior Editor Simon Beecroft
Senior Designer Robert Perry
DTP Designer Jill Bunyon
Production Nicola Torode

First American Edition, 2001

00 01 02 03 04 05 10 9 8 7 6 5 4 3 2 1

First published in the United States by DK Publishing, Inc., 95 Madison Ave., New York, NY 10016

ISBN 0-7894-7928-1

A Catalog Record is available from the Library of Congress.

Color reproduction by Colourscan, Singapore
Printed and bound by L.E.G.O., Italy

Photography credits:
All Monster Jam action photos provided courtesy of **SFX Motor Sports, Inc.** Additional non-action photography by **Al Messerschmidt:** pages 4-15 and 42-43.

See our complete catalog at

www.dk.com

GRAVE DIGGER